Hoffmann

# The Earthquake Challenge

# The BEAR GRYLLS ADVENTURES series

# The Earthquake Challenge

**Bear Grylls**

Illustrated by Emma McCann

✗ Bear
Grylls

BEAR GRYLLS ADVENTURES

First American Edition 2019
Kane Miller, A Division of EDC Publishing

First published in Great Britain in 2017 by Bear Grylls, an imprint
of Bonnier Zaffre, a Bonnier Publishing Company
Text and illustrations copyright © Bear Grylls Ventures, 2017
Illustrations by Emma McCann

For information contact:
Kane Miller, A Division of EDC Publishing
PO Box 470663
Tulsa, OK 74147-0663
**www.kanemiller.com**
**www.edcpub.com**
**www.usbornebooksandmore.com**

Library of Congress Control Number: 2018946325

Printed and bound in the United States of America
2 3 4 5 6 7 8 9 10

ISBN: 978-1-68464-040-9

*To the young survivor
reading this book for the first time.
May your eyes always be wide open
to adventure, and your heart full
of courage and determination to
see your dreams through.*

# GOT TO GO

Fatima felt snuggly and happy in her sleeping bag, until she opened her eyes.

Then she groaned softly.

She'd woken up too soon. The tent was pitch-black.

Fatima had deliberately not drunk anything after dinner. She had gone to bed a little bit thirsty, just like the night before, when she had slept soundly all through the night.

Tonight Fatima's body had other ideas.

She needed to pee.

Fatima groaned again. It was the middle of the night. But she knew she couldn't wait for morning.

She had to go.

Outside, camp was completely silent. No voices or music from any of the other tents. The only sounds she could hear were her tentmates breathing. Chloe and Sophie were fast asleep. Fatima hadn't told them that at home she still slept with a night-light on. It kept the dark-monsters in her imagination away.

Fatima silently unzipped her sleeping bag. She had gone to bed in her sweatpants and T-shirt. She felt around for her slip-on rubber clogs, her hijab and her hoodie, and put them all on. Last of all, Fatima reached for the flashlight under her pillow. Then she took a deep breath, unzipped the tent flap and stood up outside.

The flashlight's tiny little beam wasn't much comfort. It made a circle of light on the ground so that she could see where she was going, but it didn't do much to fight the rest of the darkness.

The tent clearing was surrounded by tall trees that looked like black cutout shapes of giant animals, stuck onto the sky. A slow wind made their branches shift and rustle as if the giant animals were muttering to each other.

*"See that girl down there? We are going to get her …"*

Fatima shivered, and not just because the night wind was chilly.

It was always like this.

She *tried* to remember what the place looked like in the daylight. She had used that trick before. That way, when the light was gone and the dark closed in, she could tell herself, "There isn't really anything nasty out there."

Nothing lurking.

No giant animals.

No dark-monsters.

That was what she *tried* to tell herself. But her imagination was always a whole lot more persuasive.

Without realizing it, Fatima had started walking a little faster. Her foot bumped against a guy rope, and she almost fell flat on her face. When she stumbled, something jogged in her hoodie pocket and it took her a moment to remember what it was.

Oh yes, the compass.

Yesterday she had made a new friend, a boy called Jack. He had helped her finish the orienteering course. She had been too afraid to go into a dark cave to stamp her clue sheet, and so he had done it for her. He hadn't even asked why. Fatima had been very grateful for that. And he'd rescued her map from a tree hanging over the lake.

Then, for some reason, he had given her the compass.

But a compass wasn't much use now, in the dark. Fatima could feel the dark-monsters creeping up behind her, but she didn't want to hurt herself, so she made herself slow down. But that just meant the dark-monsters started creeping up more quickly. She kept her eyes facing forward.

Fatima could see the bathrooms' outside light on the far side of the tent clearing. The closer she got to it, the more she hurried, feeling the dark closing in behind her.

Moths and insects buzzed around the outside light, but that didn't bother her. It was only the darkness that made her feel afraid. Fatima ran straight into the girls' bathroom.

The lights were always on inside. She slammed the door shut behind her and puffed her cheeks out with a heavy breath while her heart slowed down. She had made it.

She put the flashlight down by the

sinks and quickly went into a stall.

As she came out to wash her hands, she felt much better.

Then she remembered that she had to make her way back again, through the dark.

Fatima held her hands under the dryer. It whirred into action for a couple of seconds. Then …

*Fzz.* The power had gone.

The dryer stopped.

The lights went out.

The whole place was plunged into darkness. Even darker than outside. There was no moonlight here, no stars. Nothing to see by at all.

"Oh, come on!" she shouted.

It was a power cut – the thing she hated most of all when she was at home. Fatima began to imagine the dark-monsters creeping up behind her. Her heart thudded inside her chest.

"O-okay," she said out loud. "I know there's nothing there. It's all in my mind."

She felt for where she had put the flashlight by the sinks. Her trembling hand knocked against it and she heard it fall to the tiled floor. *Snap*. Something had definitely broken.

"No!" Fatima groaned. She knelt down and felt around for the flashlight. Something loose rattled inside the case when she picked it up. She flicked the switch.

And flicked it again.

Nothing.

The flashlight was broken.

Fatima bit back a scream. There was no way out of the darkness. She was trapped in the building with her head full of dark-monsters.

## 2

# IN THE DARK

The compass!

Fatima suddenly remembered Jack's present. Did it have some kind of light, maybe? Perhaps the dial would light up like a phone?

She fumbled in her pocket. The darkness felt alive around her, closing in on her. Her breath was coming in short, sharp pants. She tried to make herself breathe more slowly.

Fatima's trembling fingers closed

around the compass. She yanked it out and held it in front of her eyes.

Fatima could make out the dial – just. The directions were luminous, but there was no light-up face, no button to press. She couldn't use it as a flashlight. In fact, it was so dim that she could barely make out the directions.

Then she looked again – and for a moment it looked like there were five points on the dial, not just the usual North, South, East and West.

Strange.

Fatima gritted her teeth together, and put the compass back into her pocket.

She knew her eyes would adjust to the dark eventually. They always did. There would be tiny bits of light around the door and coming through the windows. So, eventually, she would be able to see her way out of here.

But that wasn't happening this time. *Why wasn't it happening?*

Shudders ran through Fatima's body and she forced her fears away. Okay. Okay. The room wasn't that big. She had been standing facing the sinks when the light went out. So, all she had to do was turn to her right and walk, and she would reach the door.

She turned herself around, and put her hands out in front of her. Then she summoned up every scrap of courage and started to walk into the dark.

All that her hands touched was air, and then more air. She kept shuffling along.

And then farther still. But there was no wall, no door. Was the room bigger than she remembered?

Then, thank goodness, she could see a glimmer of light. The black was turning slowly into gray. She could make out shapes.

But the shapes weren't familiar. Fatima winced as she tried to match the shapes with her memories of the bathroom in daylight.

In the far distance, Fatima thought she heard a rumble. Was it a thunderstorm? It was a long way away and it was more like she *felt* it than heard it.

Then, out of the darkness, her hands touched something strange, something soft. Fatima gasped in shock and pulled her hand away.

Whatever it was, it wasn't the wall.

It felt like *clothes*. Clothes hanging on a rack.

Weird.

Then Fatima thought she saw someone standing, a few feet to the side of her. They weren't moving.

Fatima realized it was too thin and too still to be a person.

15

It was a store mannequin. And there was another one behind it.

Then she made out racks of clothes all around her.

*"What?"* Fatima exclaimed. "Where ...? How ...?"

Fatima realized that she was no longer in the girls' bathroom at camp.

Somehow she was in a clothes store. A dark, deserted clothes store. Her mind spun. It was impossible.

Had she sleepwalked? She had heard of people doing that. But if she had somehow sleepwalked from camp into the nearest town then she had gone a very long way.

But it didn't matter how, she told herself. She still had the same problem – she had to find a way out. And she only ever came up with the same solution – keep going until you reach a wall or a door.

Fatima began to walk again.

Then she heard that rumble again. Louder, closer. It was like a train, or the main road near where she lived. The sound ran from the floor and up her legs before it reached her ears.

But then other noises started to add to it. Weird creaks and groans that she felt in her teeth and her stomach. Fatima could feel herself starting to panic again. Her legs were trembling.

Then Fatima realized it wasn't fear that made her legs do that. It was the floor. The ground really *was* shaking.

One of the clothes racks began to slide across the floor.

Then there was a *cre-e-e-a-a-k* and

suddenly part of the roof fell in. It smashed down to the floor on the other side of the room. Fatima didn't usually scream, even when she was frightened, but she screamed loudly now.

And then there was another *cre-e-e-a-a-k* … right above her. Fatima broke into a run and the shaking floor threw her from side to side. She yelled and stumbled, waving her arms around to keep upright.

A door flew open in the distance.

At last, a rectangle of daylight! She could just about make out a man standing outlined in the doorway. But Fatima didn't feel scared. Instead, she felt relief. She wasn't alone, after all.

The man spun around and spotted her.

"Take cover!" he called over to her urgently. "You need to get down on the floor, quick as you can!"

Fatima ignored him. She just wanted to get out. She started to run toward the daylight, but then the floor gave an extra hard shake and Fatima's feet disappeared from beneath her.

## 3

# AFTERSHOCK

Fatima landed on the hard ground with a thump that knocked the breath out of her. She gasped. The floor was still shaking, and she could hear the ceiling creaking above her.

The man who had been trying to help her dropped to all fours.

"Over here!" he called, as he jerked his thumb at a table that was covered with scarves. "Quick! Follow me, and stay low!"

He showed the way by crawling over to the table. Fatima followed him.

The man helped Fatima get beneath the table, to protect her from the dust and debris that was falling from above.

"Try to keep hold of the table leg," the man shouted over the din. "It will stop the table shaking away from us." Fatima grabbed hold of the table leg he pointed at while he took hold of another one.

"What's happening?" Fatima gasped.

"It's the aftershock from an earthquake," he said, fixing her with a stare that said he knew what he was doing. "And when that happens, the first two things to do are get down, and, if you're indoors, find shelter that won't fall in on you."

She could see him clearly now in the light coming through the open door. He was tall, with dark hair and a tanned face.

"Will it all fall down?" Fatima asked nervously.

"It shouldn't. They build modern buildings to stay up in an earthquake – but that doesn't stop everything inside from being thrown around."

A few seconds later, the shaking died away. The noise that sounded like a runaway train went off into the distance.

"That's probably it for the moment," said the man. "Let's get out of here."

Getting out suited Fatima just fine, despite what he had said about modern buildings not falling down. She had felt this one shaking like jello and she didn't trust it. They climbed quickly out from under the table and picked their way back to the door. Clothes racks had been shaken out of place by the quake, and just inside the door there was a cleaning cart lying on its side with brooms and buckets tumbled around.

"So, are you Suki or Anika?" the man asked. "And where are the others?"

Fatima blinked in surprise.

"Um – I'm on my own. I'm Fatima."

"Oh." It looked like it was the man's turn to be surprised.

"Okay, well, nice to meet you, Fatima. I'm Bear and I'm here to help guide you out of here." He paused. "This isn't going to be an easy journey."

He looked around, then back at her with a smile. "Are you ready for an adventure?"

Fatima looked around at the remains of the store.

"As long as we can have the adventure outside," she told him.

Bear grinned.

"Trust me, getting outside is a priority."

Together, they started to move toward the nearest door and the light. But when they stepped out, Fatima was surprised. She had thought they would be exiting the building into the outdoors.

Instead, she saw that they were in an indoor shopping mall with stores all around on multiple levels. There had been a glass roof above, but it had shattered in the earthquake. Piles of glass lay all around them on the floor.

She looked up through the open roof
above and could see daylight flooding
in.

The damage from the quake was
everywhere. An ice cream stand lay on
its side. All the tables and chairs at an
outdoor restaurant were jumbled up
everywhere.

"The earthquake hit the city badly,"
said Bear. "It's been evacuated so
everyone has left."

"So what are you doing here?" Fatima asked.

"I came to find –" he began, but then he stopped. He cocked his head like he was listening for something. "Can you hear that?" Bear asked.

Fatima strained her ears. She wasn't sure what she was listening for. So it came as a surprise when Bear put his hands to his mouth and bellowed: "HELLO!"

This time Fatima heard what he heard. It sounded like a small kid shouting back.

*"Help!"*

"It was that way," Fatima said. She pointed across the mall. Bear started walking, and once again he shouted: "HELLO!"

There was another cry. This time they could both immediately tell where it was.

"It's from in here." Bear hurried over toward a large recycling dumpster on wheels that lay on its side against a wall where it had been thrown by the quake. He thumped a hand on it, and someone inside shouted back.

Fatima gasped with horror. She couldn't imagine being trapped in one of those. It would be so dark. And how could they breathe in there? They had to get whoever was in there out, as fast as they could.

Bear tried to lift the dumpster up, heaving with all his strength. But he couldn't move it, and the lid was wedged closed.

"The lid must have

gotten bent when it toppled over. I need something to lever it with …" Bear muttered as he looked around.

"How about this?" Fatima asked.

Some of the tables had umbrellas, all furled up, and she picked one up. It was longer than she was, and she staggered a little with it until Bear took it from her.

"Smart!" he declared with a smile. "Good work."

He rammed the tip of the umbrella into the crack between the lid and the rest of the dumpster, and strained. The lid suddenly flew open. Fatima and Bear peered in.

Two small girls and a little boy peered back, blinking in the sudden light.

4

# DROP – COVER – HOLD ON

"Hi," Bear said with a friendly smile. "You're Anika, Suki and Ryan, right? I'm Bear. I promised your mom I'd come and get you. She recorded this for you."

He held up a phone. The screen showed a woman waving.

"Hi, kids. This is my friend Bear," she said. "I twisted my ankle so I can't come for you, but I'm okay. Bear said he will make sure you get to me safely. You can trust him."

"Can I talk to Mommy?" the little boy asked.

"You're Ryan, right? Not right now, little buddy. Mommy recorded that earlier. There's no signal to talk to her now."

Ryan's face started to crumple. Bear quickly hoisted him out of the dumpster and spun him around before putting him down, which distracted him and made him laugh.

"Don't worry, buddy. I know where Mommy is," Bear promised.

"I'm Anika," said the biggest girl as she climbed out. She was a bit younger than Fatima. "We waited like Mommy said, and she told us to make sure we were under cover, so when the roof started to fall in, I made us all hide in here and I closed the lid."

"Well, that was a very wise move," Bear agreed.

He lifted the smaller girl out of the dumpster.

"So, you must be Suki," he said to her. "And this is my friend Fatima, who's going to help me get you all home safely."

Fatima smiled and nodded. She was used to helping out with her little brothers and sisters.

"Sure," she said, and Bear flashed her a grateful smile.

Then Bear gathered them all together and knelt down beside them.

"Now listen carefully, team. We are going to need to work smart and work together, if we're going to get home in one piece." He paused, and looked at each of them in turn. "But it won't be easy and we will face many challenges. Do you think you are going to be able to be strong and brave enough to make it?"

They all nodded and Ryan and Suki jumped up and down shouting, "Easy peasy!"

"Then let's do this! Okay," Bear said, "first up, we're in the middle of a badly damaged city. We can't trust any building to stay upright. There's no clean water to drink, or electricity to keep us warm and give us light. We're on our own." Their smiles and enthusiasm rapidly turned into worried looks. "But our priorities are just the same as if we were out in the wild somewhere – protection, rescue, water and food."

The kids were all ears as Bear went on.

"Like I've told Fatima, there may be

more aftershocks. If that happens, the rules are drop, cover and hold on. *Drop*, so you don't hurt yourself by falling."

Bear dropped quickly to the ground to demonstrate, and the kids laughed. He got back up and dusted himself down with a smile.

"*Cover* means get under something

that will protect you from falling stuff. Maybe a table – or a big trash can!"

Anika laughed.

"And *hold on* means just that," Bear continued. "Your shelter will be shaking around just like you, so you need to keep it with you – like we did with the table, Fatima."

He looked around at them all.

"Now, our first job is to get everything we need together. And as we're in a shopping mall that shouldn't be hard. We'll start over there."

Bear pointed to a sports store, but frowned when he glanced down at their feet. The store was on the far side of a sea of broken glass. Fatima was only wearing rubber clogs, with open backs, and the kids had flip-flops and sandals.

Bear was wearing leather boots that were scuffed but which looked tough.

That meant that only he could walk across all the glass safely.

"I could carry you, I suppose …" he thought out loud.

"Hang on," Fatima said. "I know just the thing!"

She ducked quickly back into the clothes store behind them. What she needed was right by the door, in the light. There was the cleaning cart – and a broom with a nice wide head. Bear smiled when he saw it.

"Perfect! Okay, everyone, follow me and walk exactly where I walk."

And so they all walked across the mall in single file,

with Bear pushing the broom in front to brush the broken glass aside.

Fatima had never thought that just walking across a mall could be an adventure. The city had been built to be a safe place for humans. The quake had turned it against them.

At first Fatima hung back at the entrance to the sports store. It was dark and she would rather stay in the daylight.

But the sports store had bigger windows than the clothes store, so it wasn't quite as dark inside. And they could see even better when Bear found some flashlights and batteries.

Finding boots for them all took a while because none of the younger kids knew their shoe sizes. Fatima had to help them by guessing what their sizes were, and then picking out the labels on the shoeboxes with the flashlight.

Bear made sure they all chose boots made of tough leather with good solid treads underneath. He also picked out some fleece pullovers, light waterproof jackets, and hats for everyone, and gave them each a backpack and a tough plastic sports bottle. The kids all looked like it was their birthday as they proudly wore their brand-new stuff. He added some cooking gear – pans and plates – to his own backpack.

Bear added up the cost of everything they had taken, and left some money tucked under the register to pay for it all.

"Always be honest. Just because we are in an emergency doesn't mean we lose our morals," he explained. "We do what is right. Always. Now, let's find an exit."

Fatima studied a map of the

shopping mall outside the sports store. The mall was shaped like a big cross, and they were down one of the arms.

"The nearest exit's this way," Fatima said, pointing at the end of the next arm. She remembered Bear's list of priorities for a survivor: *protection, rescue, water, food.* "And there's a supermarket on the way, so we can get supplies there."

"Good girl, Fatima." Bear looked proudly at her. "Just like being in the wild – you need to plan your way ahead as much as you can."

They all walked down to the center

of the mall. Anika and Suki held hands. Fatima held Ryan's hand, not just to comfort him but to stop him slipping on the broken glass that was everywhere. She felt the glass crunch beneath their feet and was extra grateful for the tough footwear.

The little group turned right toward the exit – and Fatima stopped in dismay.

"Oh."

Most of the mall had been left standing by the quake – but not this part. At the far end there was just a pile of rubble.

And there was no sign of a way out.

5

# EXIT STRATEGY

"Oh, no!" Suki burst into tears. Anika was putting on a brave face. Ryan hadn't quite worked out what this meant.

"It's okay," Fatima said quickly. "There must be another way out. Right, Bear?"

"In a big place like this? There's bound to be," Bear agreed, with a smile to show the kids he wasn't worried. "But first things first. Let's stock up on supplies. Fatima, bring the team and help me."

The supermarket was the last store

before the enormous pile of rubble. Fatima gulped and swallowed as they all stood in the entrance. The lines of shelves disappeared into the darkness. She could imagine dark-monsters lurking at the back, just out of sight.

Bear waved his flashlight, making crazy shadows jump around. Cans, bottles and boxes lay on the floor. When he ran the beam over the ceiling, Fatima could see pipes and metal bars through square black holes where roof tiles had fallen down. Some of the ceiling lights had come loose and dangled from their cables.

Fatima did *not* want to go into the darkness and the shadows. But she had to be brave, for the kids' sake. Bear had asked her to help him.

They moved slowly into the store. There were lines of abandoned shopping carts and baskets at the registers, all full of shopping. When the quake had hit, people must have just left their carts and run. Bear picked through the things in the nearest one. "Milk – already gone off. Frozen pizza – also gone off, and we couldn't cook it easily on a campfire anyway. Soft drinks – let's pass on those. They just make you thirstier than when you began. We'll do our own shopping.

"Anika and Suki, and Fatima and Ryan – you each get an empty cart of your own. Stick together in pairs. I'll keep this one."

"*Three* shopping carts?" said Suki.

"That's a lot of shopping," Anika added.

"They're not all for shopping," Bear said. Fatima remembered his talk about the earthquake drill, and she immediately guessed what he meant.

"If there's an aftershock while we're in the store," she said, "we turn our carts upside down and hide under them."

Bear smiled and nodded.

"You've got it. There may be more stuff falling from the ceiling, or cans dropping off shelves," he said. "You'll be safer inside a metal cage. Okay, team, let's do this."

They moved through the store in single file with their three carts. Fatima let Ryan sit in the seat on hers. Their

47

flashlights lit the way down the aisles and light reflected back off the shelves – but Fatima could imagine dark-monsters in the aisles on either side, pacing along to keep track of the little group.

Bear picked up some packages of energy bars, and lots of cans of tuna and baked beans.

"Small, easy to carry and you can eat them hot or cold," he said cheerfully.

"Also they'll pack in the energy when we eat them, and they're something to look forward to. Let's get something to wash it all down with."

In the drinks section

he found several large bottles of spring water.

"Okay," Bear said, "let's see your nice new sports bottles, shall we?"

He lined their bottles up in his cart, and began to pour the bottled water into them.

"Mommy says bottled water is a rip-off," said Suki.

"Well, it can be," Bear agreed as the water glugged into Fatima's bottle. "It's a luxury, really, because it costs about three hundred times more to take it out of the ground and put it in a plastic bottle than it does to just drink it out of the faucet. But, here and now, we can't trust what's in the faucet. The quake could have cracked pipes open and it could all be mixed up with sewage. So bottled water is safer."

Ryan tugged at Fatima's sleeve.

"What's sewage?" he asked.

"It's what goes down the toilet," she told him.

*"Yuck!"*

Fatima smiled – not just at Ryan's reaction but because now they would be heading out into the daylight again. It was so dark and her heart was beating so fast in here. She couldn't wait to get outside.

So when Bear walked farther into the supermarket, her heart sank. He pointed his flashlight over the signs on the ceiling.

"One more thing ..."

Bear had found the pharmacy section. He took a couple of boxes of bandages off the shelves, and rummaged through the other bottles and packages.

"Got it!" Bear sounded pleased with something he had found. He held up a small bottle. "Potassium permanganate. Very useful for disinfecting cuts, purifying water ..." Bear was on a roll now, grabbing things off the shelf as fast as he could. "And also let's get some tape and some blister bandages. Just in case. Okay, let's go."

They wheeled their shopping carts back to the entrance, where Bear again left some money for everything they had taken. Fatima sighed deeply with relief to be back outside in the daylight.

*Finally! No more hanging around in that dark place!*

Bear unpacked his cart into everyone's backpacks. He distributed it all according to how big they were, so that he ended up carrying the most and Ryan had his water bottle and a single can, which he was very proud of.

"And now let's find our way out of here!"

They headed back to the map of the mall and crowded around it. Bear pointed with a broken pen that he had spotted lying on the floor, and showed the group where they were on the diagram.

Then he traced the way to the blocked exit.

"So we can't go that way. Which means …"

He frowned as he moved his pen back and forth across the map, searching for another route out. But there were no other exits marked.

It seemed that there was only one way in or out of the mall, and that way was blocked by a hundred tons of rubble.

# 6

# ROOFTOP VIEW

All the children turned and looked up at Bear questioningly.

Bear knew this wasn't looking good.

"Could we move the pile? Bit by bit?" Fatima asked. "I mean, we could put the bricks in the shopping carts and wheel them away?"

"I'm just a bit wary of disturbing it," Bear told her. "You don't know what else might then come crashing down. Let's try to find another way. All these stores must have fire exits." He jerked a thumb back at the supermarket.

The kids seemed okay with that, but Fatima felt it like a thump in her stomach.

There was nothing wrong with Bear's plan ... except for one thing.

*Go back into that big, dark, empty place? We just got out of there!*

Bear seemed to notice something. He took her gently to one side.

"You okay, Fatima?" he asked in a quiet voice.

Fatima wanted to say "I'm fine," because that was what she always did. She had never admitted it to anyone but her parents – but then no one had ever needed her help like Bear did.

He deserved to know the truth.

Saying it out loud felt like the bravest

thing she had ever done.

"I'm really afraid of the dark," she whispered.

Fatima braced herself to hear all the usual stuff like: "stop being silly," "there's nothing to be scared of" and "that's childish."

But Bear surprised her.

"I can understand that," he murmured. "I expect you've heard it all before, right?" he asked. "You've no doubt told yourself it's all in your head, it's not real …"

Fatima nodded.

"It doesn't help," she said.

"Well, admitting there's a problem is always the first step to fixing anything. And you've done that, which is such a big step for you. But, you see …"

Bear tapped his head with a finger.

"The victory starts in the same place as the fear. Up here. Your brain is amazing and it's there to help you. You just need to start learning how to get your thoughts and emotions to work for you rather than against you."

"I can't, and they don't." Fatima still couldn't speak louder than a whisper. She looked at the dark entrance to the supermarket. "I just know that I can't walk all the way through that place again."

"You don't have to do it all at once. But you do have to stop expecting a negative response. Stop feeding the fear. You can do this and your brain can help you. You are going to tell yourself that it is an irrational fear and that you are not going to let that fear dictate how you live. Okay?"

"Okay. Sort of. But how do I do that?"

"Well, firstly, know that the fear isn't based on truth and then make a decision to walk toward it." Bear paused to let his advice sink in. Then he continued. "Together, we will take one positive step toward the fear, toward the dark. We will do it with courage, and when we feel the fear rising we are going to tell it to back away, and then we are going to keep going."

He smiled as he saw a mix of excitement and trepidation building in Fatima's eyes.

"And then once we have done that, we do it again. And again. Until the fear goes away and your control of the situation grows. Because all those positive steps will add up."

Bear looked right at her. "Can you do it?"

Fatima looked at the floor and then up at him – and she nodded.

"Good for you, Fatima. This is how you are going to conquer your fear." He paused. "I can't do it for you. But you can do it."

Fatima smiled nervously.

They went back into the supermarket. There were grumbles from the girls.

Only Ryan seemed happy because he could shine his flashlight around.

At first it wasn't so bad. They had been here before. But this time they pressed on through, all the way to the back. Bear led them through a door and it was like going into a dark maze. Storerooms, offices and more corridors. Fatima hadn't realized there were so many spaces in a supermarket.

Her heart thudded inside her so strongly. She wanted to run away as fast as she could, but she forced herself to keep walking. She held on to Ryan's hand and kept going. One foot in front of the other, just like Bear had said.

Fatima kept telling herself that the

fear had no power over her, and that by moving forward and kicking the fear away each time it rose up, she could do this.

And it was actually working.

Eventually they came to a solid door with a metal bar across it and the words FIRE EXIT printed above it in red letters. Fatima imagined all the lovely sunshine on the other side and felt relief wash over her.

"Okay, here goes!"

Bear pushed on the bar and the door swung open … into a dark concrete passage. Fatima's heart plummeted.

Bear's flashlight beam played over a pile of rubble farther along, where the ceiling had fallen in.

But then his flashlight lit up a flight of metal stairs at the end of the passage.

"I'll bet those will take us all the way up to the roof – and chances are good there'll be a metal ladder or a fire escape down the outside of the building."

The group edged their way forward into the darkness. Ever farther.

The stairs took them up a square concrete stairwell. Into the darkest place yet. They moved upward in their beam of light. Fatima's heart thudded inside her, but she kept doing as she had done before – she just kept going.

Another solid door blocked their way at the top. Bear rammed his shoulder against it and it flew open!

The kids cheered as daylight flooded into the stairwell. Fatima breathed a sigh of pure happiness.

Bear winked at her. "I knew you could do it." He peered around.

"Everyone hold hands with Fatima or me until I'm sure it's safe."

Fatima quickly realized why Bear wanted to hold the kids back.

"There's the fire escape!" Suki shouted.

Fatima had to pull Suki and Ryan back as they both suddenly tried to run across the flat roof.

A railing ran all the way around the roof. Right across from them there was a gap, and Fatima could see the top of some metal stairs.

The staircase went all the way down to the ground – but there was a small gap between the top stair and the building. The quake had torn it away from the wall.

Bear approached it cautiously, and prodded it with his boot. It creaked and groaned and wobbled.

"Not that way," Bear decided. "Our weight could pull it off the building altogether. We'll find another way down, but while we're up here, let's take the opportunity to plan our journey. The main priority is to get out of town and meet up with your families."

Fatima looked out at the city. Quake damage was everywhere. In one direction she could see a whole bunch of tall buildings and skyscrapers. Most of the windows were broken and some office buildings had cracks running up them. That was probably the city center.

"So –" she pointed in the opposite direction – "we want to head that way?"

Bear smiled and nodded.

"Yes. Toward the main road out of town. That's our priority. Head west. Okay, let's see how to get down."

The small group patrolled slowly around the edge of the roof.

But there were no other fire escapes. The nearest building was maybe fifteen feet away – way too far to jump.

They were back where they had started. Fatima thought through their options.

"So the only way down is a fire escape that is too dangerous to use, or …" She swallowed nervously. "Or go back into the building?"

Bear looked around the roof, and smiled.

"Or," he said, "we climb down!"

## 7

# HOSE HARNESS

"Climb?" Fatima asked in surprise.

He surely didn't mean climb down the dangerous stairs.

She took a peek over the railing that ran around the top of the building and down the wall. It was smooth bricks. It would be impossible to find handholds on a wall like that. And it was a *long* way down.

Fatima looked around the roof. It wasn't completely flat or empty. There were pipes, and cables, and machines that looked like giant fans inside metal cages.

And then she saw it.

A sign saying FIRE HOSE above a glass case, which was fixed to the wall next to the door where they had come out. A hose was curled up inside it.

Bear was already on it. He smashed the glass with a hammer clipped to the wall, and started to pull the hose so that it unreeled onto the roof.

"We're about sixty feet off the

ground," he said seriously, "and it says this is seventy-five feet long. I'll make a harness and lower you one by one. Fatima, I'll be holding on at this end, and I'm going to need someone to look after the kids on the ground, so are you okay to go first?"

"Um – sure," Fatima said. "But I'm heavier than them," she added. "Can you hold my weight?"

"I won't be holding anyone's weight. I have a plan. Don't worry!"

By now all of the hose was uncoiled on the roof. Bear dragged it all over to the railing and looped one end of the hose around it. Then he looped it around once more.

"The railing will be like a pulley that takes your weight, and then I just have to hold the hose and let you down gently," he said. "Taking a double wrap around it means it will be easier for me to lower you."

Bear started to tie a loop in the hose at the other end.

"Classic bowline knot," Bear said. "Make a loop, then the end is like a rabbit that comes out of the hole, around the tree and back down the hole!" As he spoke he threaded the hose in the way he described, with the end of the hose acting as the rabbit.

Fatima perked up. "I remember learning that knot in scouts!"

"Nice! Well, now's the time to test it! Put your arms through here, so it's under your armpits, and then lower your arms to your side to trap the hose."

Fatima did as Bear instructed. "Keep your armpits clamped to your sides," he added, as he tightened the bowline around her. "Now hold the hose in front of you and don't let go. You ready for this?"

"Ready!" she said with newfound confidence.

Butterflies still fluttered in Fatima's stomach as she climbed backward over the railing and hung over the four-story drop, but she knew she had conquered her fears before, and she knew she could do it again.

"Don't look down," Bear said. "Just keep your eyes on the wall in front of you and your armpits tight. Push your legs out against the wall so you aren't hanging just on the hose. Ready? Here goes."

The wall began to move slowly past Fatima's eyes.

It was a smooth, steady ride down to the ground, as she slowly walked backward down the sheer face of the wall. The hose ran smoothly over the railing and Bear could take her weight with no problem. In no time at all Fatima felt her boots touch the ground.

She wriggled out of the harness and stood back so that Bear could pull it back up. While he was doing that, Fatima looked around.

The city felt eerie with no one else around. Cities were meant to be full of noise. Usually there were cars and people, alarms and trains, and airplanes flying overhead. The noise was just *there*, even if your brain tuned it out.

You only really noticed it when it wasn't there anymore. Every movement she made, even her breathing, seemed to echo. It was weird, but it wasn't frightening – in the daylight.

But Fatima gulped as she thought ahead. She didn't know what time it was, but she could see it was past midday. The sun was starting its journey down toward the horizon, and she guessed they would still be in the city as night fell. They would have to find somewhere to sleep.

It would be silent, and it would be *dark*.

*No!* she told herself firmly. *Don't think like that.*

She would cross that bridge when she came to it. She would conquer her fear, again and again, until it lost all its grip on her, like Bear had said. She smiled to herself. She was sounding like a survivor.

Suki came down next, with her eyes squeezed tightly shut. She even kept them closed while Fatima helped her out of the harness, until she could actually believe she was on solid ground.

Then came Ryan, then Anika, and last of all Bear himself. He looped the hose over himself, just like the others had, but he held the end that was wrapped twice around the railings in his hands. Then he slowly started to lower himself down the wall.

"Great work, team!" Bear smiled around at them as he touched down on the ground. "Right, let's find an open space, away from anything that might decide to fall on us, and then I think we've all earned a quick drink before we push on."

They walked toward the shopping mall's parking lot. It was wonderful to finally have the big dark building behind them.

But after only a few feet, Fatima heard a noise like an approaching train.

She had heard it before ...

"It's another aftershock!" Bear called.

In another half second the ground began to tremble.

Bear dropped down to all fours. "Everyone, down on the ground!"

## 8

# CAR CAMP

*Drop – cover – hold on!* That was what Bear had told them before.

Fatima pulled Ryan down to join her on the ground as bits fell off the mall building with loud crashes. But *drop* was all they could do. The only *cover* was the abandoned cars on the other side of the parking lot, too far away to run to. And there was nothing to *hold on* to at all.

"Curl up!" Bear called. "Protect your head and neck with your hands, like this."

He curled into the tightest ball he could, with his hands over his head. Then he uncurled and made sure the girls were doing it, while Fatima looked after Ryan.

Glass shattered and metal crunched as the shock rocked the abandoned cars. The asphalt felt gritty and sticky, and it stank of gasoline and oil. Fatima could hear everything creaking and groaning. She felt like a bug curled up on the ground that could be squished at any moment.

But the rumbling died away and Fatima uncurled slowly. There were fresh cracks in the walls of the mall building, and a haze of dust and dirt in the air.

But everything was now still again.

They gathered themselves together and moved off as a group.

No one spoke much
and there was tension in
the air.

They knew an aftershock
could hit again at any time.

Bear tried to lighten the mood and
insisted they all have a picnic together,
sitting on a bench at a bus stop. Everyone
snacked on an energy bar and washed
it down with water. It was a hot, sunny
day, and Fatima had made sure everyone
wore their new hats from the sports store
to protect their heads and necks from
the heat. *Bear isn't the only one who
knows how to survive*, she thought
to herself with a smile.

Then they started to walk.

The little group hiked for a
couple of hours. Suki and Ryan

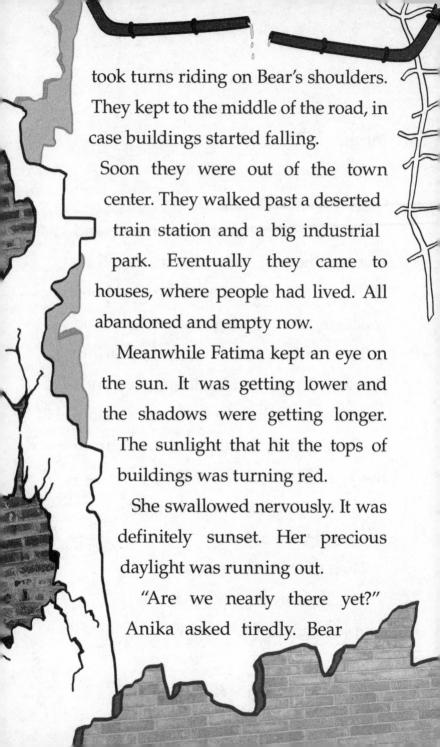

took turns riding on Bear's shoulders. They kept to the middle of the road, in case buildings started falling.

Soon they were out of the town center. They walked past a deserted train station and a big industrial park. Eventually they came to houses, where people had lived. All abandoned and empty now.

Meanwhile Fatima kept an eye on the sun. It was getting lower and the shadows were getting longer. The sunlight that hit the tops of buildings was turning red.

She swallowed nervously. It was definitely sunset. Her precious daylight was running out.

"Are we nearly there yet?" Anika asked tiredly. Bear

smiled gently and told her what Fatima had already guessed.

"We're going to have to camp out tonight, but we should be back with your mom before lunch tomorrow. She's in a temporary hospital where they are fixing her foot, but she'll feel a whole lot better the moment she sees you all."

Bear called a halt when they reached a small park with a children's playground, surrounded by stores and houses. Next to it were two cars that must have once been neatly parked on the street. Now they were both turned upside down, having been thrown around like toys by the earthquake.

"We can't drive these damaged cars, but they are perfect shelter," Bear said. "They're a steel shell that will protect us, and keep the weather and scavengers out."

"What's a scavenger?" Suki asked.

"It's an animal," Anika told her.

"Kind of," Bear agreed. "It's any animal looking for free food. Dogs, cats, urban foxes – they'll all be used to humans feeding them. Now that the humans have gone, they'll be looking for food on their own – and they won't all be friendly."

While the kids played on the swings, Bear and Fatima checked the cars for leaking oil and gas – anything that could catch fire or be unsafe.

"You and the kids can

sleep in one," Bear suggested to Fatima. "And I can take this other one."

The roofs inside both cars were big, flat surfaces that would work fine as beds to lie on. But they would need something to protect themselves from the cold ground below.

"Cut up the seats, and get the foam out of them," Bear said to Fatima. "You can use it as insulation tonight, to stop the ground sucking all the warmth away. I'll make us a fire."

*Trusted with a knife!* Fatima thought with a smile. Her mom would have a fit. But she knew Bear well enough by now to understand that if he trusted her to be smart with a task then she would live up to the challenge.

She took the knife and got to work.

By the time she had finished Bear had collected some dead branches from the bushes in the park. Then he got some bandages out of his backpack and made a small pile on a concrete slab. Next he took out the bottle of potassium permanganate he had found in the supermarket, and poured some onto the bandages. Last of all he took a bottle of antifreeze that he had found in the trunk of one of the cars, and poured it over the pile.

He waited a few seconds ...

*Whoomph!* The whole pile of

$KMnO_4$

bandages caught fire.

They all whooped with delight at the fire in front of them.

Bear grinned.

"That's potassium permanganate reacting with glycerin in the antifreeze – my favorite chemical reaction! Pretty cool, eh? But to keep it burning, we need fuel."

He started to put the dead branches on top of the fire, one by one, and they began to burn too.

They sat on some cushions that Bear had found in the back of one of the cars, with picnic blankets wrapped around them. Bear heated baked beans and tuna in a metal saucepan over the flames, and then dealt out their helpings onto plastic plates. Fatima hadn't realized how hungry she was until she started to wolf it all down with a plastic fork. The day's adventures had really taken it out of her.

By now the sun had gone completely. Darkness rushed in over the city, right up to their tiny circle of firelight. Shadows closed in and peered over their shoulders.

Fatima turned her back on them and made herself focus on the fire, and on her friends. She had light and she had company.

Bear was eating with the rest of them, but he kept looking around for scavengers. And that was why Bear was the first one to see the light.

"Look," he said. "Over there."

Some distance away there was a single beam of light shining up into the sky.

"What is it?" Fatima asked.

"It could be a signal," Bear said. "Maybe there's someone trapped there – someone who needs help." He made a face. "I have to go and see who it is. Fatima, I'll have to leave you here, in charge."

"Me?" Fatima said in alarm. She had just begun feeling safe and secure, but suddenly all that vanished.

Bear smiled and lowered his voice so that only she could hear.

"Keep stepping up to the challenge, Fatima," he said. "You've got this. You are doing so well, girl. But someone else needs help and I should go …"

"Um. I guess." Fatima swallowed, but she nodded.

She was going to be on her own, with three small children to care for, and no Bear, and darkness all around her.

# FATIMA IN CHARGE

Fatima wanted to call out, "Come back!" as Bear disappeared into the darkness.

But Bear had told her she could manage, and the children already looked a little bit frightened. She didn't want to let Bear or the kids down. Bear had believed in her before, and she had proved she could do it …

No. There was no way she would let them down by giving up.

"Okay," Fatima said instead. "Who knows any songs?"

And so they taught each other different songs that they knew. It made a happy sound and it pushed the dark back a little bit. Bear had cut a small pile of sticks, and whenever the fire went down Fatima put another one on the flames. The fire picked up again and the darkness stayed back.

Then something moved at the edge of the light. Fatima gasped as two yellow eyes stared at her.

But half a second later, the owner of the eyes came into view. It was a black-and-white cat. The three children were immediately all over it. It purred loudly and seemed especially interested in Ryan's leftover tuna.

Suddenly a loud *crash* came out of the dark, and everyone jumped. A building that had been damaged by the quake chose that exact moment to collapse.

"Wow!" Fatima gasped. "Okay, is everyone all right?"

"Ryan, no!" Anika shouted.

Fatima spun around. She had been facing the fire, so it took a moment for her eyes to adjust to the dark. But by then Ryan was gone.

So was the cat. It had spooked at the noise, and Ryan had run after it. Fatima heard him in the distance, shouting, and caught glimpses of Ryan's flashlight shining around.

*"Catty, come back!"*

"Ryan!" Fatima yelled. But there was no reply.

Suki was crying for her brother, and Anika looked terrified.

Fatima knew she had to find Ryan. He might get lost, or run into some aggressive scavenger.

"Right," she said firmly. She thought, hard. First thing was to take care of the girls. "I have to go and get Ryan. Bear has to know where you are when he gets back, and you have to stay safe – so I want you both to get into the car, so you can look after each other and I can concentrate on finding your brother."

Suki and Anika nodded nervously, but they climbed in.

Fatima looked around, remembering something she'd learned in scouts. She grabbed an upturned shopping cart that was lying nearby and put it on top

97

of the car. "This will help Bear know where you are," she shouted as she worked. "It will act as a distinct marker in case he can't find you if I'm still away." She paused. "Now keep calm, all right? I won't be long. Hang tight. Be brave!" And with that she ran off to find Ryan.

"Right," she muttered to herself as she ran. "Scavengers or not, here I come …"

She knew that there would be hungry animals looking for food. *And they won't all be friendly*, Bear had said. She needed to be able to defend herself.

Fatima remembered seeing a wrench

earlier when they had been looking through the cars. It was used for changing tires. She soon found it again. It was a solid metal bar about twelve inches long with a little arm on the end.

She hefted it in one hand and held the flashlight in the other. Then she followed the direction Ryan had gone.

Her ears picked out the occasional shout of "Cat!" from ahead. Ryan didn't sound frightened. He just wanted his furry friend back.

The sounds led Fatima away from

the park. She was on her own now – in the dark.

"Ryan! Come back here!" She kept shouting as she hurried toward the glimpses of his flashlight in the distance.

Fatima kept her light focused ahead so that she didn't trip or bump into anything that could hurt her. She could see only what was ahead, the rest was all darkness. She kept calling Ryan as she went. The only noise was the sound of her footsteps echoing back from the walls.

Then she rounded a corner and the light from her flashlight lit up Ryan.

"Ryan! Wait right there!" She raced over toward him.

"Ryan … there you are!" she breathed with relief.

They were in a small square. Ryan was standing alone, pointing his flashlight up toward a ledge. His face was heartbroken.

"Cat went up there," he said. Fatima flicked the flashlight beam at the ledge, but there was no sign of it.

"I expect it's gone back to its friends," she said. "Shall we go back too?"

Ryan pouted.

"Want the cat."

"Well, we've still got some tuna. Maybe the cat will come back for that?" He looked at her hopefully. She pushed the point again. "Cats always remember where food is, and they can smell it from a long way off."

"Okay," Ryan grumbled.

They made their way back through the dark to the park, guided by the flickering lights from their flashlights. The girls had gotten out of the car and were sitting next to the fire again when they got back. Fatima was about to tell them off when she saw that Bear had come back too.

"Hi, there!" he called when he saw Fatima's flashlight. "The girls said you'd gone to get Ryan. All okay?" He ruffled Ryan's hair, then looked at Fatima.

"Well done, you," he said with a sincere smile. "That can't have been easy, but you did everything right. Protected the girls, marked where they were ..." He glanced at the shopping cart on the top of the upside-down vehicle. "And then protected yourself." This time he looked at the wrench in her hand. "Smart girl. And brave."

Fatima felt kind of embarrassed by his praise.

"Well," she said, "I just …" Her voice trailed off as she realized something.

*She hadn't been beaten by the dark. A little scared maybe, but definitely less so than before. She had persevered and not given up.*

She had been more scared that Ryan might get hurt than she was by any imaginary monsters.

*Wow.*

"Did you find anyone?" she asked, to change the subject.

Bear shook his head.

"It was just an automatic security light, battery powered. Well, we should all turn in. Why not help the kids settle down?"

"Sure," Fatima agreed.

She knelt down to open the car door. It was stuck. She gave the handle a big pull

and tumbled backward
as it flew open. Fatima looked
around.

The park had gone. She was no
longer in the city.

"Bear?" she asked. She looked around.
"Ryan? Anika? Suki?"

They were all gone. She was back at
camp, outside the door to the bathroom.

How had she gotten back here?

Had she been sleepwalking and had a
really weird dream?

Fatima automatically began to head
back toward her tent because it was
chilly and there was no sense in hanging
around. She had picked her way through

the tents and guy ropes, halfway back, when she realized something once more.

She wasn't afraid. Well, that was one thing she *had* brought back with her from the city. From now on, imaginary dangers were just ... well, imaginary.

Fatima looked up. There were no clouds, which meant she could see the stars.

Thousands of them. *Millions.* Pinpricks of light as far as she could see. And there was the Milky Way – a band of light that ran from one side of the sky to the other.

This was the dark, and it was truly beautiful.

10

# CLEANUP CREW

"Fatima, wake up!"

Her tentmate Chloe was fully dressed.

"You'll miss breakfast if you sleep any longer!" Chloe said. "Remember we're on cleanup today."

"Oops!"

Fatima sat up quickly and looked around.

It was daytime and the tent was full of light. Sophie had already gotten up and gone.

"Come on," Chloe said, "I'll see you there!"

She slipped out of the tent, leaving Fatima alone.

Fatima got dressed quickly and went out into the daylight. She stretched wide and let out a big yawn.

After that really weird sleepwalking dream thing last night, Fatima had just sat and stared at the night sky for ages. It had been *awesome*. Eventually she had made herself go back inside the tent because she had known she needed some sleep.

And now she needed food, so she hurried after everyone else.

Breakfast was served on picnic tables outside the food tent. It was a busy scene, with a camp full of kids all jostling to get their helpings of cereal, toast, eggs, and everything else that was available. It was always a good start to the day.

But it had to be cleaned up afterward. Every camper was put onto a cleanup team for one meal during camp, and this morning it was Fatima's turn to help. The leader in charge gathered them and checked their names off a list.

"And you're Fatima," he said, "so that's everyone except ... Has anyone seen Charlie?"

"Charlie? Charlie!" everyone called.

Charlie was still sitting at a table, with his head over his tablet while his fingers moved against the screen. He looked up with a sudden guilty expression.

"Oh, sorry ... hang on ..." he said.

His head went back down.

"Charlie," the leader called, "*now!* Put that away."

Charlie grumpily came over to them. He still held on to the tablet, so he hadn't actually put it away.

"Right," the leader said with a smile. "Let's get started. Gather up all the plates and cutlery, uneaten food goes into one of the bags, cutlery goes into this basket here …"

And so they got to work.

Most of them.

Fatima and Charlie started on opposite sides of one of the long tables, piling everything up.

By the time Fatima was halfway down her side, she realized she was way ahead. Charlie was playing his game again.

"Charlie!" Fatima sounded more impatient than she had meant to.

Charlie scowled. Maybe because they were the same age, he was less polite to her than he had been to the leader.

"Sorry, *Mom*," he said sarcastically.

Charlie just squished all the plates on his side into a pile, one on top of the other, and then went back to his screen.

Fatima sighed. He wasn't exactly being very kind or helpful – she thought about all the things she'd had to do to keep safe with Bear and the kids in the city. Bear would have reunited the children with their mom by now. Charlie really didn't know how lucky he was here at camp.

"Come on, Charlie," she said gently. "You're meant to scrape the food off first."

"You do it then," Charlie snapped back angrily, as he went back to his game.

But their conversation had gotten the leader's attention. He made Charlie hand over his tablet, so that he didn't have a choice about helping.

"That is so unfair!" he complained as he started stacking the plates. He was obviously annoyed as he crashed them together.

Fatima thought again about her strange dream last night.

Bear had helped her face up to the

dark, hadn't he? She reckoned that Bear would be able to find the right words to help Charlie start doing his bit and to get positively involved. But how could she get Charlie into her dream?

She smiled sadly. *That* wasn't going to happen.

Fatima had built up a big pile of plates to carry over to the kitchen. She thought about asking for Charlie's help, but she didn't want to be snapped at again, so she dug her fingers under the pile and lifted them.

The bottom plate was slippery with ketchup and her fingers couldn't get a grip. With horror, Fatima felt the whole pile slide through her hands and land on her feet.

"Fatima!" the leader gasped as he hurried over. "Are you okay?"

Fatima stared down. Nothing hurt. Some of the plates had broken, but her feet were totally fine.

"Y-yes," she said, surprised. "I'm fine, thanks." But any other words just dried up in her mouth as she realized what she was looking at.

Charlie came running over. His sulk had vanished.

He squinted at her feet.

"Lucky you were wearing those boots," he commented. "It could have really hurt otherwise." He paused. "You okay?"

"Yes. I'm fine," Fatima murmured, still in a daze. "And, uh, thanks, Charlie."

Fatima stared at her feet.

If those plates had fallen on her rubber clogs, she would definitely have been hurt. The pile had been heavy.

But she was wearing a sturdy pair of boots. She had put them on without thinking when she left the tent in a hurry.

They were the very same walking boots Bear had gotten for her in the sports store in the mall.

It *hadn't* been a dream.

Fatima got through the rest of the clean-up with her head still spinning. At the end everyone was meant to go off to their activities for the morning. But Fatima sat at one of the tables, deep in thought.

How had she gotten to the mall? She had left the tent in the dark to use the bathroom. She had gone into the bathroom. The lights went out. And then … what?

Her thoughts were interrupted by electronic squeaks and squawks. She looked around and realized Charlie had also stayed behind. He had his game back and was sitting at the end of the table with his head in another universe.

*Sometimes,* Fatima thought, *Charlie was perfectly friendly. But he seemed to change the moment he got his game back.*

Fatima got up to go, but then she felt the compass in her pocket.

The compass! Of course! She remembered that had been weird last night. It had seemed to have five directions, right before she found herself in the clothes store.

Was it the compass that did it? Maybe the compass could take Charlie to Bear?

Well, nothing ventured, nothing gained.

"Hey, Charlie?" she said. "Want to see something cool?"

"Mm?" He didn't look up, so she put the compass on the table next to him. He picked it up and squinted at it.

"What does it do?" he asked, puzzled.

Fatima smiled.

"Perhaps you'll find out?" she said. "Just consider it a gift."

### The End

Bear Grylls got the taste for adventure at a young age from his father, a former Royal Marine. After school, Bear joined the Reserve SAS, then went on to become one of the youngest people ever to climb Mount Everest, just two years after breaking his back in three places during a parachute jump.

Among other adventures he has led expeditions to the Arctic and the Antarctic, crossed oceans and set world records in skydiving and paragliding.

Bear is also a bestselling author and the host of television programs such as *Survival School* and *The Island*.

He has shared his survival skills with people all over the world, and has taken many famous movie stars and sports stars on adventures – and even President Barack Obama!

Bear Grylls is Chief Scout to the UK Scouting Association, encouraging young people to have great adventures, follow their dreams and to look after their friends. Bear is also honorary Colonel to the Royal Marine Commandos.

When Bear's not traveling the world, he lives with his wife and three sons on a barge in London, or on an island off the coast of Wales.

Find out more at **www.beargrylls.com**